Story by Rudy Wiebe

Paintings by Michael Lonechild

RED DEER PRESS

Sky Running is looking for buffalo. All day he has looked, but he has seen none.

He eats prairie-rose petals. They are moist on his tongue and gentle as honey. All day he has eaten nothing else, while he carefully searches the prairie from the high hill his Cree People call The Nose.

Sky looks west, and south, and east to the bright flash of Sounding Lake where he can see the tips of his home tepees. The wide land lies below him, endless grass and folds of creeks, into the distance where earth and sky meet. Nothing moves.

In this autumn Moon of Changing Leaves the prairie around Sounding Lake is always black with buffalo—cows with their calves playing near them, the bearded bulls itching themselves against rubbing stones and roaring.

Sky knows that their hunters must find buffalo, so his People can eat now, and dry the meat for food in the coming winter. But during all the moons of summer they have found no animals. Where have they gone?

Slowly the day is ending. Sky raises his arms high to honor the sun burning red on the rim of the earth. Then he runs. Down the ravines of the long hill, stripping the last purple saskatoon berries from their bush as he passes.

This evening their family has a little food. Mother and Auntie have dug up wild turnips, and Father has hunted a badger. They eat the good stew, holding each mouthful to make it last as long as possible.

Sky gives his handful of saskatoons to Little Sister and their two cousins. They eat the berries very carefully, one by one, and Auntie smiles at him.

Grandmother is old, and she can only walk bent using a tall stick. But her voice is strong, and full of stories.

"When the Creator made the world," she tells them, "he showed People food for every season. The sweet sap inside poplar bark in spring. Turnip roots to cook in summer. Prairie-rose hips for chewing in autumn after their petals fall.

"That was very good, but the wise Creator knew winter snow was cold. People would freeze to death unless he gave them meat."

"So, hidden deep under water in the ground, the Creator made great herds of buffalo. He said to them, 'People living on earth are hungry. If you are kind and give them your meat to eat, I promise that you will always have many strong calves.'"

Grandmother tells this story every year, but now Sky hears her voice slowly rise, as if she were singing a prayer.

"And the buffalo cried, 'Oh, yes, yes!' and up into the light and air they burst. It was here they came up for us, out of the ground from under the water, and the sound of their coming was like thunder rolling.

"That is why we call this water Sounding Lake."

Little Sister is crying quietly. "But where are the buffalo now?" she asks. "I'm hungry."

Grandmother says softly, "I think the buffalo are still here. But they are hidden. We need more powerful eyes to see them."

Sky walks along Sounding Lake. On the water, the moonlight flakes a path like prairie snow drifting.

He shivers. He wants to feel the buffalo thunder under the earth, to hear their sound as they burst up, to see them running on the moonlight.

The lake chuckles as softly as his heart beating. Suddenly the rich taste of buffalo steak fills his mouth, and he swallows hard. But his mouth is empty, dry. He walks until he is standing still.

He lifts his hands to the sky.

"O Great Creator," he sings, "I am so hungry."

By his left foot at the edge of the water is a white stone. He picks it up. It feels cool, and smooth as rubbing fur. He opens his fingers. A white stone buffalo lying in his hand.

The lodge is filled with the sounds of People sleeping. When Sky slips under the sleeping robes, Grandmother touches his hand. Sky gives her what he has found.

Grandmother grumbles deep in her chest, like buffalo talking. Then she folds Sky's hands tightly around the stone.

Sky whispers, "We can't eat stone."

Grandmother grumbles again. "You can keep it warm," she says.

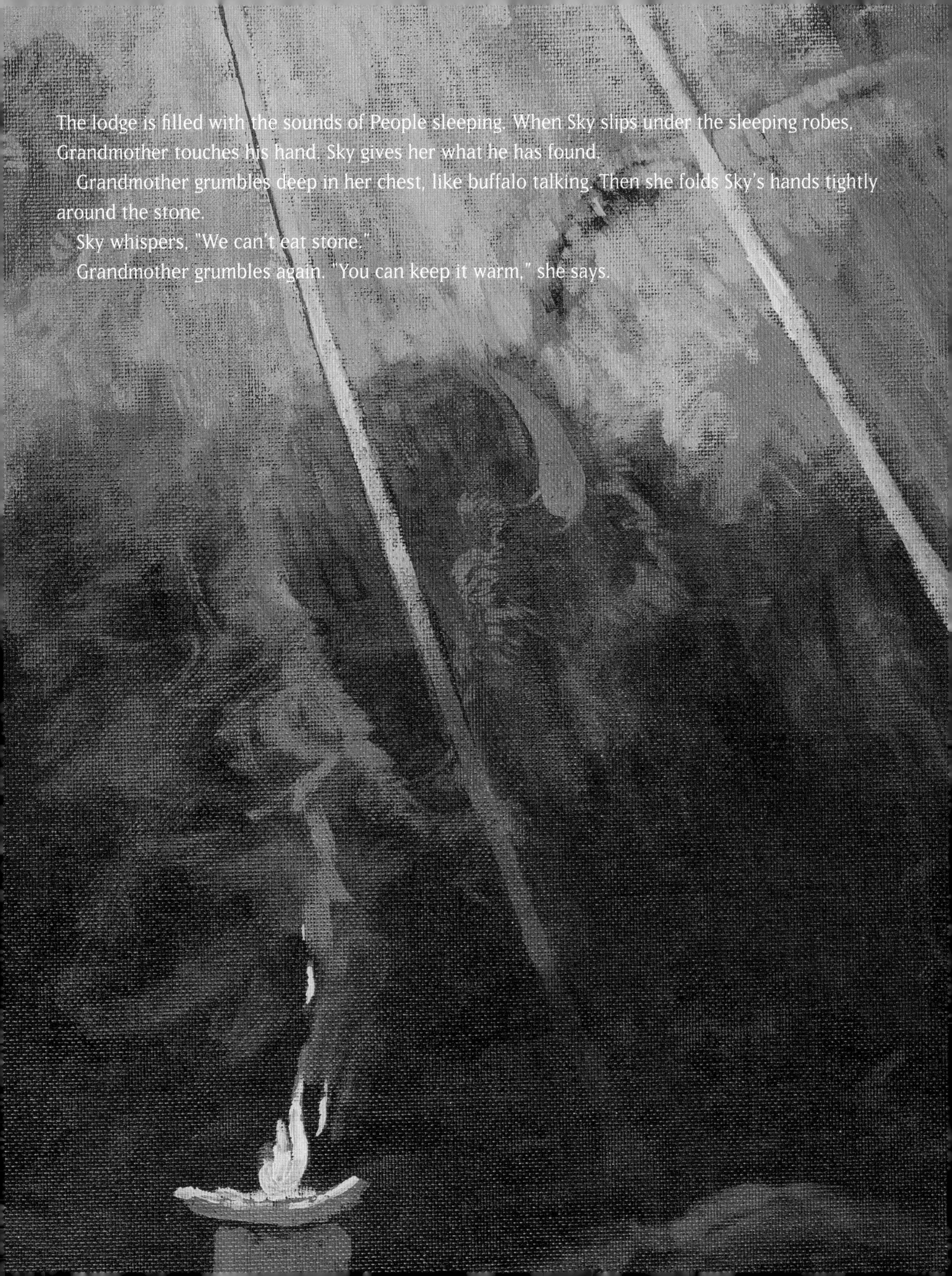

Sky feels the thick body, the hump, the bending head. Then he is asleep, quick as falling.

And he sees the earth has opened below him, like a huge mouth wide and deep, and there they are. The hidden buffalo, so many he cannot see an end to them.

Sky looks all around with great care, and he sees that the earth rises high over them in layers of black and light brown and white cliffs. Like painted steps to lead his People down to the beautiful animals grazing there, between the giant loops of a curling river.

Sky is awake. The lodge is filled with daylight and his whole family is staring at him.

Little Sister tells him, "You were laughing out loud."

But Sky cannot speak. He can only whisper to Grandmother, who becomes very serious. "We must tell the People," she says.

When the Chief and the People see the white buffalo stone and hear Sky tell what he has seen, they are all worried.

The Chief says, "Where the earth goes down in painted steps is far away. Those are the Badlands, along the Red Deer River, in the land of the Siksika People. That is too dangerous for us."

Sky's mother stands up. "We must go where the buffalo are," she says. "Our children cry for food."

"But those People are our fierce enemies!"

Grandmother speaks: "I think Siksika also have children. If we meet, we could tell them where the buffalo are."

The Cree People are travelling south. Their long caravan spreads out over the dry prairie, three hundred children and men and women carrying packs and walking. Dog and horse travois haul their lodges, their cooking pots, their sleeping robes, everything they need to live.

Sky is so tired, his pack so heavy. Grasshoppers skirr as he forces his feet through crunching grass. But on a trek everyone must be careful.

He looks up. Beside him Grandmother rides a horse travois, holding her stick. And far ahead he sees the young men on their fast horses. Scouts lead them on, alert for any danger.

They meet no Siksika. After four days of hard travel under the autumn sun, the People come to the place where suddenly the prairie falls away in painted steps. From high along the cliff they look down into the earth. And there, between the giant loops of the river, the valley below them is black with numberless buffalo.

Sky's father comes to him leading a white horse.

"The Chief invites you to come," his father tells him, "and ride with the hunters. Here is a horse for running buffalo."

Sky cannot speak for happiness. Little Sister and his two cousins dance around him.

"O buffalo, O sweet, sweet buffalo!" they sing.

All the People stand facing the sun. With hands high and open they thank the Creator, who again has given them the immeasurable gift of food.

And then, with Sky Running in the lead, the hunters ride down into the earth to the buffalo.

Published in the United States in 2004
First published in paperback, 2006

5 4 3 2

NORTHERN LIGHTS BOOKS FOR CHILDREN ARE PUBLISHED BY
Red Deer Press
A Fitzhenry & Whiteside Company
1512, 1800–4 Street S.W.
Calgary Alberta Canada T2S 2S5
www.reddeerpress.com

CREDITS
Edited for the Press by Peter Carver
Cover and text design by Ben Kunz, Kunz Design
Printed and bound in Hong Kong for Red Deer Press

ACKNOWLEDGMENTS
Financial support provided by the Canada Council, the Department of Canadian Heritage, the Alberta Foundation for the Arts, a beneficiary of the Lottery Fund of the Government of Alberta, and the University of Calgary.

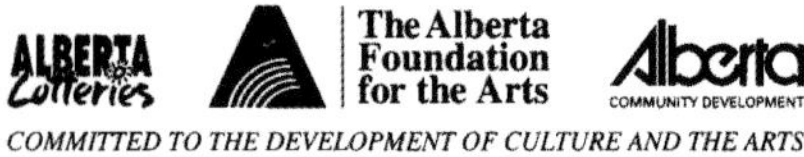

Canadä

THE CANADA COUNCIL FOR THE ARTS SINCE 1957 | LE CONSEIL DES ARTS DU CANADA DEPUIS 1957

NATIONAL LIBRARY OF CANADA CATALOGUING IN PUBLICATION DATA
Wiebe, Rudy, 1934–
Hidden buffalo / Rudy Wiebe; Michael Lonechild, illustrator.
(Northern lights books for children)
ISBN 0-88995-334-1
I. Lonechild, Michael. II. Title. III. Series.
PS8545.I38H52 2003 jC813'.54 C2003-910450-8
PZ7.W635Hi 2003